Schloss Valkuriz

A NOVEL BY

Felicia N. Cheung

Schloss Valkuriz
Copyright © 2020, 2010 Felicia N. Cheung
Second edition
First published 2010

Cover rose image: Tiger Images / Shutterstock.com
Cover background image (HB1): Banthita166 / Shutterstock.com
Cover background image (HB2): tomertu / Shutterstock.com

HB1 ISBN: 978-1-64713-158-6
HB2 ISBN: 978-1-64713-159-3

Printed in the United States of America

For my dearest father
Michael Cheung Kwok Ching
(1949 - 2017)

I love you very much, dad. You are forever in my heart. May you rest in the sweet arms of Jesus Christ, your loving Savior, and may you enjoy all the pleasures of Heaven, your eternal home.

Contents

Chapter 1. A Glimpse of the Past

Chapter 2. A Flame Ignited

Chapter 3. The Promise of the Rose

Chapter 4. The Stranger in the Woods

Chapter 5. Twilight

Chapter 6. A Starless Night

Chapter 7. Affairs of the Heart

Chapter 8. Pleasure and Pain

Chapter 9. A Declaration of Love

Chapter 10. A Brutal Assignment

Chapter 11. A Dark Secret

Chapter 12. A Strange Message

Chapter 13. Shadows of the Past

Chapter 14. Faded

Chapter 15. The Parting

Chapter 16. The Isle of Hope

Chapter 17. A Valkuriz Sonata

Chapter 18. The Essence of the Rose

I

A Glimpse of the Past

London, 1829

he gentleman standing by the mantelpiece laughed amiably as he brushed a stray wisp of hair from his eyes before taking a sip of champagne. He was not like any other man Iara had ever encountered. As he stood there conversing with the host in the luxuriously furnished drawing room of Hayden Court, she perceived that there was something very special about him, something altogether striking. Perhaps it was his exquisite beauty, his aura of grace and sophistication, his distinct manner of authority or simply the allure of his charming smile. He was arrayed in splendor and elegance and in his eyes danced the stars of the empyrean.

Whenever he turned his head, all eyes turned towards him, battling desperately to be the sole object of his gaze. Whenever he looked away, all eyes sighed with melancholy and sought to indulge their fancy in the meantime by gazing upon his imposing form. The gentleman, however, exuded an air of nonchalance and expressed scant regard for all this attention as he was accustomed to being so esteemed in society. He only offered a courteous smile whenever his eyes met the eyes of one of his admirers and actually stayed long enough to warrant an acknowledgement on his part, a gesture which was more than sufficient to produce in the latter a sensation of euphoria and give hope to others on whom his eyes had yet to lay.

Iara sat down at the pianoforte and with great flair and finesse, flooded the room with a classical piece she had composed. It was a haunting melody yet beauteous and elegiac in its rendition, a song which soon attracted the gentleman's attention for shortly after she began playing, he cast a brief glance in her direction before turning back to his partner and resuming his conversation. A casual glance it was, accompanied by neither smile nor acknowledgement, but it was a glance nonetheless and like many others before her, Iara secretly wished that the gentleman would look once more in her direction. At length, he parted with his companion and made his way towards her.

He addressed her, saying, "If I may, my lady, I desire the pleasure of making your acquaintance." He spoke with a subtle German accent yet exhibited a superb mastery of the English language, the tone and modulation of his voice laced with the utmost eloquence and charm.

Iara rose to her feet, executed an elegant curtsy, and said, "I understand that you are our honored guest this evening, Your Lordship."

"I believe your father wants to introduce his daughter to me. But I requested and have been granted permission to carry out this formality myself," said the gentleman, "What is your name?"

"Iara Suri."

"I'm very much inclined to dance right now, Miss Suri," he said whereupon he extended to her an invitation to dance with him.

"Yes, gladly," she replied, taking his hand.

"You are a very graceful dancer," he said as they started to dance, "Tell me, how do you find the country?"

"Very delightful indeed," answered Iara, "The country has its own charms. I am especially fond of strolling through the beautiful countryside."

He followed this by asking, "Then might I be so bold as to persuade you to visit the country on my account?" And perceiving the look of incomprehension on the young lady's face, he added, "Will you visit me at my castle in Leicestershire?"

"Visit you at your castle? But we've scarcely been acquainted, sir. Propriety forbids it."

"Pray forgive my impertinence, ma'am," replied the gentleman, "I spoke out of haste. How very unlike me to do so!

You must now think me the object of incivility."

"Far from it, sir. Should I be flattered by your invitation?"

"I would wish so," was the response. And it gratified him to hear her say that she was indeed flattered.

"What is Schloss Valkuriz like?" asked Iara.

"A dreamer's paradise, Miss Suri," he answered, smiling, "Now do you wish me to bend the rules of conduct for you once more, my lady?"

Iara had encountered many gentlemen in her lifetime but none so suave as the dashing young lord of Schloss Valkuriz. Were his fortune to be reduced tenfold and his looks reduced likewise, she would still find him the most handsome person she had ever laid eyes upon. He had the voice of an angel; the very words uttered from his lips were infused with unquestionable warmth and kindness and reminded her of an angel she saw when she was a child. And thus in the midst of her romantic reverie, she found herself musing on her own past.

Her joyous countenance had been disturbed by a dire adversity, one that had denied all possibilities of escape. In the wake of this impending tragedy, Iara held unto the hope that had sustained her and swore a solemn oath of renewed strength in spite of her situation. Life had given abundantly and likewise had taken away so much so that she was now left empty-handed. Yet she was rich with the many sorrows that defined her existence and the only thing wanting was to sheathe the cruel blade with her youthful flesh. For the first time in her life, she grasped fully the rewards of untimely quietus. She longed to kiss death's ashen cheeks, to hold death's ashen hands, and to feel the touch of life everlasting.

And in this manner, she witnessed the angel of death coming towards her with arms open and a welcoming smile. She let the dark angel hold her and felt consoled by his presence. She smiled a sorrowful, fading smile but one that put forth all the rejoicing of its possessor and even more joy now for her despair would soon give way to perpetual happiness and to this end, her spirit was uplifted. It wasn't the angel of death, however, who cradled her in his arms but an angel of mercy in the guise of a man in possession of a saintly soul and whom she thenceforth knew as her guardian angel. And in the comfort of the night, she was satisfied with the knowledge that all her pains would be duly recompensed by virtue of her renewed and steadfast faith in Christ.

She was put under the instruction and tutelage of a very accomplished governess who was as devoted to Iara as the young lady was to her own education. When the hours of school had ended, she would ensconce herself under the cool shade of the trees, basking in serenity and there she would peruse countless volumes written by authors of classical lore until the light of the sun no longer shared her passion. The sun shed its brilliant rays upon the flowing strands of her hair so that the wavy locks boasted radiance upon a sea of shimmering ebony. Blessed with stunning beauty and elegance, she was both envied and admired by the fair among her acquaintance. Wisdom and common sense formed the principal features of her intellectual design wherein she enjoyed a sense of power coveted by those in want of such trait. And her experience in overcoming hardships untold added to her character the fortitude and resilience necessary to sustain her whenever past sorrows resurfaced.

Happiness, however, was not always a loyal companion and the burdens that awaited its absence placed themselves all too keenly upon her. Oftentimes she had been the victim of a restless slumber where the veil of reality gradually lost its essence and when the cover of sleep was at last laid upon her and the shadows of the night were slowly closing in, she found herself at the mercy of dark dreams. And though her dreams were mostly horrific, she was soon haunted by the recurrence of one that resurrected in her a passion now forgotten.

II

A Flame Ignited

A note addressed to Iara:

*D*ear Miss Suri,
  Please be so kind as to allow me to express my sincere gratitude for the pleasure of your society at the evening ball hosted by your dear father and if I may be so bold, madam, to request your company at my castle for the duration of an extended visit. Should you respond in the affirmative, I will furnish you with a barouche for your journey once I receive your answer in writing. Regardless of your reply, I respect your decision and I thank you in advance for your prompt and honest response. Please do me the honor of accepting my invitation.

Faithfully yours,
Nikolas Kessler

FELICIA N. CHEUNG

Her reply to the above:

Dear Sir,

I thank you most graciously for your kind invitation. I am very pleased to confirm my acceptance and I look forward to visiting you at Schloss Valkuriz.

Sincerely,
Iara Suri

Lord Nikolas Kessler was twenty-nine years of age and an aristocrat of impeccable lineage who was not only blessed with a strikingly handsome visage but had also achieved numerous honors and accomplishments throughout his life. An expert in the art of war, he served first as a soldier in the imperial court of Austria and from there he quickly ascended the ranks of the military. His rapid accumulation of wealth, procured both through his own assiduity and through the munificence of his superiors, allowed him to purchase one of the stateliest castles in England immediately upon his resignation from the Austrian court. Though a decidedly powerful and influential personage throughout the region and its adjoining areas, he maintained a dignified and courteous air towards all he encountered, a quality which earned him an excellent repute among nobility and gentry alike. He was therefore highly regarded in society and as many believed, one of the very few gentlemen who truly deserved the favor bestowed upon him.

*T*he quaint countryside in which the castle of Schloss Valkuriz lay possessed a quiet charm and distinctive air within its borders wherein the luxuries of its surroundings lay bare. Adorned by picturesque forests on all sides, the castle stood in the heart of Leicestershire and seemed to be the centerpiece of all creation. Even the sun seemed to shine more brilliantly on this part of the country, so much more so that the schloss was constantly bathed in the refulgence of a thousand rays. The rare flora and exotic verdure that blossomed there gave the whole a feeling of precious awe.

The sun began to set as the carriage approached the gates of Schloss Valkuriz. Iara was received by Mrs. Harcourt, the housekeeper, who led her into the drawing room of the castle. A colossal painting in an elaborately gilded frame hung above the mantelpiece in the drawing room. The portrait showed two men standing together as brothers. The gentleman standing on the left was Lord Kessler, arrayed as a military general of the Austrian court. Beside him was a gentleman of Asian descent dressed in the uniform of an Austrian soldier and bearing equal beauty and stature.

"This painting is one of my master's most treasured possessions," said Mrs. Harcourt, "It was commissioned by the king of Austria himself and presented to Lord Kessler at court in recognition of his great services."

"He is the very picture of sophistication and dignity," observed Iara as she gazed upon his image, enraptured by it. Her gaze soon shifted to the soldier standing beside him. His face seemed somewhat familiar as if she had known him in a previous lifetime but any such recollection eluded her at that moment. Yet there was something about him that moved her and carried her to a realm in which life had promised endless joy. The curious desire to ascertain truths contained in the portrait led her to enquire the identity of the gentleman.

"He was my master's dearest friend," answered Mrs. Harcourt, "It's all very mysterious what had transpired that fateful night. Lord Kessler keeps all this to himself, you know. His friends know only that the soldier standing beside him was his dearest friend and that his passing has cast a perpetual shadow over his life."

"Did they not inquire further?" asked Iara.

"Yes, but all their questions were met only with vague answers and as time passed, such questions and the spirit of curiosity that generated them gradually faded," replied the housekeeper. With that, she left the room.

Iara closed her eyes and in the incandescent white light, glimpsed the picture of the familiar stranger to whom she played admirer for in that portrait, she knew a thousand longings. *Who is that man? His face, I've seen it before… countless times in my mind, in my dreams…* Shadows of fear surrounded her and she felt herself strangled by the clutches of the dark. Then she saw Lord Kessler emerge from these shadows and felt herself observing him, studying his form with great admiration. And being thus engaged, she hardly noticed him entering the room and was aware of his presence only when he gave voice.

"A gift from His Imperial Majesty, a memento of my days at court."

"Good evening, sir," said Iara, "Schloss Valkuriz is a most splendid castle indeed; it far surpasses any I've seen."

Lord Kessler smiled in response and sauntered across the room towards her. He gave her a decorous kiss on the cheek and said, "Welcome to Schloss Valkuriz, Miss Suri." The scent of perfumed musk emanated from his body, the crisp aroma sweeping the air around him as he walked. It was a very soft fragrance yet sensuously masculine, infused with a hint of sophistication and a touch of grace.

He declared, the champagne glistening in the glass as he gently stirred it, "Before you came, this place was a dreamer's paradise where I was the dreamer but now it is a palace of beauty and you reign as queen."

Iara blushed. "You flatter me, really."

"I speak only as I see it," said the gentleman, and observing the flush of rose suffusing her face, asked, "Do I make you uncomfortable?"

She replied, "No, of course not."

"How was your journey here?"

"Very pleasant indeed," answered Iara.

"I was afraid you would not accept my invitation," he said, "I'm glad you did."

"Why would I not accept your invitation?"

"Because," began the gentleman, "Propriety forbids it. We have only just been acquainted and hardly know each other. Is that not so, my lady?"

"You tease me by echoing my sentiments?"

Lord Kessler laughed. "Tease me in return then," he said, "Come, Miss Suri, I give you that liberty."

"A liberty which I must deny for I can never tease you," said Iara.

"Why not?" he asked.

"Because I've already made up my mind to commend you," she replied, "And while my words may have painted a cold picture of indifference, my heart…" Here she paused for lack of courage and the gentleman, who had thus far been watching her with the utmost attention and diligence, drew closer towards her.

Gazing into her eyes – his filled with passion and admiration and hers likewise – he said softly, as though a gentle breeze were carrying the words, "I believe a flame has been ignited, Miss Suri." With that, he smiled and drank the last sip of champagne in his glass.

III

The Promise of the Rose

The other residents of Schloss Valkuriz – Mr. and Mrs. Ingram, Mr. Vartan, and Miss Preston – were of an agreeable and pleasant disposition altogether and their longstanding friendship with Lord Kessler constituted fair grounds upon which Iara's immediate perception of their character was founded. Their regard for her was likewise solidified through their mutual respect and affection for Lord Kessler and their firm conviction that he would only invite worthy ladies to his schloss and consequently, they received her with a great degree of warmth and cordiality.

"I am eighteen, ma'am," said Iara when Mrs. Ingram enquired her age.

"Such a sweet age to be, my dear. How I wish I could turn back the hands of time so that I can experience that blissful age once more," said Mrs. Ingram, a woman of sweet temperament who took upon herself the task of being mother to all the young persons of her acquaintance. She wore around her neck a fine adornment of precious stones and the softly defined features of her countenance, preserved under a thick layer of powder and rouge, masked her true age. Her husband, by contrast, wore his age with deference and displayed it particularly well on a certain spot on his forehead where he had suffered a permanent injury while on a hunting expedition in North Africa many years ago, a mark which served as a noble reminder of one of the most cherished moments of his life since it was there that the self-proclaimed champion of hunting had met his match.

And in the air of one accustomed to the impracticalities of nature, he declared, "Yes, I should like to travel back in time too. Perhaps I'd revisit Africa. Such a marvelous and exotic place it is!"

"If I could turn back the hands of time, I would prove myself a hero by saving a life," said the gentleman sitting beside him.

"And whose dear life would you save, may I ask?" This question was posed by Miss Preston, an uncommonly tall and slender lady with an engaging profile whose speech and deportment carried a most refined air. Such refinement was conscientiously preserved by a carefully guarded and reserved tongue and through continuous improvement of the fine arts, the latter being a rather superfluous endeavor since she was already extremely accomplished at the pianoforte and the harp, had achieved complete proficiency in both

French and Italian, and her singing, dancing, painting, and fine embroidery skills were nonpareil.

"A woman I once doted on," replied the gentleman, "She took her own life to prove her love to me when mine faltered. I confess it was my fault. I dared her to do so."

Mr. Vartan was an aristocrat by birth and the rightful heir to a large estate in Derbyshire. His vast fortune, the entire sum of which had been lavished upon him by his parents and the rest acquired through inheritance, awarded him the liberty of pursuing a very carefree and reckless existence, much to the envy of his peers. Ravishing good looks, youth, and affluence were his most loyal companions for they were instrumental in his securing the hearts of countless women, a significant portion of whom he had encountered in the less salubrious areas of town where he frequently engaged in drunken revels. Why Lord Kessler would attach himself to a man of such immoral and disdainful character, however, eluded Iara's comprehension entirely but to be fair, his manners were tolerable at the very least and the crude utterances that emerged from his untamed lips forgivable since they were never directed at her.

"It's a beautiful thing, to die for love," remarked Iara, "I dare say, sacrifice is the noblest form of love."

Lord Kessler nodded in agreement and smiled as he held up his glass to her.

*T*he quiet of the night was shattered by the turbulent storm that now fell upon the land, streaks of lightning continually adorning the skies, accompanied by thunderous applause. The trees shook violently in sustained fear while relentless winds blew viciously across the fields. Iara tore open the curtains and staring out at the picture of doom, found the perfect solace in peaceful contemplation; to reflect on Lord Kessler was to attain calm amidst the heightened terrors of the night.

The tempestuous night would pass and the wondrous sun would pour its blessings upon the new morn. Iara would awaken by the first light of dawn and would walk through the halls of the castle with a sense of collected impatience. The servants would greet her with their usual civility and would inform her that their master was waiting for her in the morning room. She would feel her heart throbbing inside of her and in her overwhelming enthusiasm to reunite with him, she would forget to smile. She would enter the room before her arrival was announced and would see Lord Kessler seated at the table with a glass of champagne in his hand. He would put down the glass upon seeing her and rise from his chair. He would bow politely and receive her with his usual charm and she would remember to smile this time. Without saying a word, he would fold her in his arms and instantly, all disquiet and angst within her would be completely erased as happiness and comfort took over. *Lord Kessler, my angel...*

In the midst of the raging turbulence, Iara perceived a sense of calm as the violent thrashing of the storm gave way to the tranquil cover of sleep. That night, she saw an episode of her life revealed in an evanescent dream and with her was her lover.

Handsome and charming he was to her, just as he had been when they were together. She saw that sad look in his eyes, the look which had pierced her heart a thousand times over and had strived to cause a like expression in hers. She felt the warmth of his touch, his arms around her in a loving embrace and his fingers gently caressing her body. This night was not like other nights as this one promised new grief in a manner unfamiliar to her.

"Stay with me tonight, darling," Iara said as he embraced her passionately in a last attempt to give comfort.

"I can't, my love," he said, "I gave my word and now I must act on it. He is waiting for me. I must go to him forthwith."

"Will you not ask him, plead with him even, to release you from this charge?" she asked.

"Impossible," he replied, "He is intent on drawing blood and there's nothing anyone can do to soften his heart."

She ran her fingers through his dark hair and kissed him. "My tears shall not cease to fall until I am in your arms again," she told him.

"Sweetheart, I have a present for you," he said, handing her a velvet cloth. Wrapped inside the cloth was a beautiful red rose. The rose gleamed brilliantly in the moonlight, its crimson glow a testament to the passion that held the two lovers together.

"How beautiful," remarked Iara.

"When I visited the marketplace in Prague, I happened upon an ancient woman who claimed to know the story of my life and the path that lay ahead of me," said Lieutenant Vidur, "She gave me this rose as a gift in honor of our latest victory at court and told me to give it to the lady who possesses my heart so that she would be blessed with everlasting happiness. It is a sacred flower endowed with lasting beauty and immortality. Iara, you are the love of my life and the woman of my dreams. This rose that has been expressly given to me is now yours and I give it to you with all of my heart. Its beauty shall be sustained by the precious memories we share and its life nourished by the faithfulness of the love you bear me. Keep this rose as a token of our love; as long as you hold unto it, our love will not fade."

Holding Iara's face in his hands, he kissed her on the lips then said, "Blessings follows me because you are in my heart and so long as you cherish the memory of us, our love will transcend all things. Wait for me, my princess."

IV

The Stranger in the Woods

The weather not being the least bit inclement that morning was more than ideal for fox-hunting as had been predicted by Mr. Ingram the day before. The hunting party, most of whom were avid members of the sporting club to which Mr. Ingram belonged, gathered in the forest an hour after breakfast. One such gentleman among them was Mr. Bradford, a man of great expectations and little tolerance whose sense of accomplishment exceeded his actual worth or so it seemed. His innate arrogance and condescension towards others, particularly those of inferior rank, compelled him to associate with only the most respectable men of the gentry. Women, on the other hand, were not judged by such strict standards. A ladylike figure and an attractive visage were the hallmarks of a woman's beauty in his eyes while those admirable traits which existed within played no part in his assessment of her worth seeing as he himself possessed no such qualities.

He had learned during a recent discussion with Mr. Ingram of a new arrival at Schloss Valkuriz. The visitor, he was told, was a lady of exceptional beauty and intellect but who had no interest whatsoever in the fine art of hunting, a fact which obviously did not affect his desire to make the lady's acquaintance. And on the day of the hunt, he appeared in a stylish coat of blue superfine along with a pair of glossy hessians since first impressions were always significant in determining later opinions. He made small talk with those nearby before being introduced to the young lady.

"Miss Suri," he said, one hand resting atop his fancy cane of polished wood and the other fixed on the lapel of his coat as if posing for a portrait to be presented to the world, "I am told by my friend here that you are excellent at the pianoforte. I am, you could say, a connoisseur of classical music myself and would love to hear you play sometime."

"I assure you, Mr. Ingram has greatly exaggerated my talent, sir," Iara said.

"Nonsense!" returned the gentleman, "So you shall play for me then?"

She answered in the affirmative and declared that he would hear her play at their next meeting. He was satisfied and removed himself to join the others just as the hunt was about to begin.

Lord Kessler approached Iara and stood beside her and her heart was greatly soothed. Though he was reluctant to leave her side, he was soon forced to do so upon Mr. Ingram's insistence that he take part in the chase on the grounds that there were already many wooded trees in the forest and he need not add to the lot. Mr. Ingram further prevailed upon him by informing him that the prospect of encountering danger in that part of the forest was less than minimal. Knowing that Lord Kessler found delight in the sport, Iara too urged him to join the hunt and assured him that she would come to no harm whatsoever. And so he did, albeit with much hesitance.

Amid the great excitement of the hunt, Iara discerned a voice calling softly to her, a voice she had not heard in a long time, a voice very near and dear to her heart. She knew the voice, knew the manner with which it had called her name. The voice was sweet and angelic and somehow seemed to emanate from within her. She followed the voice into the woods, utterly lost in a trance. As she wandered deeper and deeper into the thick of the forest, the sounds of the hunt began to fade.

Somewhere in the distance, the rustling of dry leaves whispered under her feet and a tingling sense of fear crept upon her. Iara stood frozen in her tracks as a gray wolf emerged from behind a thick shrub. It advanced towards her, its eyes stalking her every movement and its legs poised, ready to prance. She closed her eyes and felt a sense of unconsciousness as her body touched the ground.

Shadows danced upon shadows, like flickering specs of light in the distance. Iara watched the faceless forms move amongst the trees, watched their shapes bend over the wandering stream. She saw the sun peering over the trees and gazed at it, mesmerized by its mystique and beauty. Then she saw him. She glimpsed the figure of a man in military attire appear behind the wolf. A stranger he was yet there was something in his mien that evoked a sense of affinity.

Who is this man who stands before me? He comes to me now in my time of peril to rescue me from the fangs of this savage beast. He is like a dream to me, real yet illusory. His very soul speaks to me. Hark! Listen carefully, listen to the silence he speaks.

As he drew closer, she realized that he was the same gentleman who had invaded her dreams on countless occasions. Her dreams, how long had it been since she last dreamt? She had no recollection of any of the dreams she had the previous nights, not since she first came to Schloss Valkuriz, not since she first met Lord Kessler.

The stranger turned towards the wolf, his hand resting on the hilt of his sword. He glanced at Iara and put a finger to his lips then signaled her to remain still. Without a moment's hesitation, he drew his sword as he began to quicken his pace. Then with a swiftness of foot that defied reality, he lunged at the animal, slashing its throat with the sword. She had seen such prowess before, had witnessed such compassion in the slaying and such heartfelt resolution to save another. Such precise and accurate timing, such agility and quickness of foot, such passion in the eyes. Those eyes, they were so telling yet she could decipher nothing of their secrets. What words were written in their eloquent glances? What truth did they deliver? What hopes transcended their mere forms? A soldier of the royal army, the pride of a prestigious court, the champion of millions across the nation, the jewel of her heart. Her heart, what was the rhythm of this organ? What music was written in its melody? What memories were concealed in its form?

The stranger wiped the blood off the blade then replaced the sword in its scabbard. He glanced at Iara once more then turned to leave. There was something peculiar in his manner of leaving, something she knew too well: the way his hand leaned on the hilt of his sword as he slowly turned from her and began walking away; the way he hesitated at first then turned slightly just to catch a last glimpse of her; the way his eyes communicated sorrow while promising happiness; the way he carried on walking, never to look back again.

Iara closed her eyes and hoped to dream once more. But he was gone. The shadows vanished altogether, their forms converging toward an invisible sphere of nothingness. When she opened her eyes, she saw Lord Kessler standing before her, a dagger gripped in his hand and his hands stained with the blood of the dead animal.

"What happened?" she asked.

"You don't know?" he said, "Why did you come here?"

"I heard a voice, the voice of a stranger," she answered, "It led me here. I saw him slay the wolf before me. And then he disappeared into the shadows."

"Who?"

"I don't know."

"You don't know?"

She shook her head.

"It's alright," said Lord Kessler, helping her to her feet, "You're safe now." A shadow of despair fell upon his countenance as his eyes roamed the woods around them.

V

Twilight

The library housed an impressive array of literary works from every era. Iara browsed through the myriad volumes standing on the shelves and selected a copy of *The Iliad*. The myths and legends of ancient civilizations fascinated her and transported her to the world of the ancient Greeks and Romans. As she read the daring exploits of those storied men of antiquity, she reflected on the atrocities of the illustrious Achaeans and felt sympathy for the hosts of Ilium. She pitied the young Paris whose naive declaration of love for the beautiful Helen had sounded the alarm for battle which led to the fall of Troy. In Achilles, she saw a fierceness that shouted arrogance and demanded glory which, in its lust for revenge, destroyed in brute manner the sacredness of human life. And in this instance, the heroic figure of the princely Hector stood above the triumphant Achilles as he struggled in his last attempt to draw breath.

"Your library is filled with historical literature," said Iara to Lord Kessler as they ambled through the lush gardens of Schloss Valkuriz, "Even the very walls of this castle are decorated with the art of past eras. I find such passion most enthralling. Are these designs inspired by your own interests?"

"We share a mutual fascination for the days of yore," he stated, "I studied classical antiquity in my youth and was versed in Greek and Latin."

"I once taught myself Latin, believing I would visit Rome someday."

"And have you visited Rome?"

"In my dreams I have," replied Iara.

"I envy you in this regard," said Lord Kessler, "Do you usually dream of such times?"

"No, such luxury is not mine."

"And of what nature are the rest?"

"Of a nightmarish sort mostly," she answered, "For as long as I can recall, my sleep has been plagued with nightmares in which even the most innocent of dreams threatened to kindle fear in me with their careful display of horror. The night we met at Hayden Court, I had a disturbing dream."

"Tell me the dream you had that night."

"A demon appeared to me in the guise of a baby. It emerged at the foot of my bed and crawled its way up my body towards me. Its grotesque body was hideously malformed and so terrifying to behold that I saw its image even when I shut my eyes. Its skin was grievously disfigured as if seared by acute fire and in its eyes lurked unspeakable evil. With the sharp claws attached to the ends of its deviant fingers, it proceeded to tear at my stomach in all directions, scraping the surface of my skin until it was covered with fresh bruises. Glaring at me with misshapen eyes, it continued to scratch my skin with its claws, unresponsive to any effort on my part to cast it away.

"All this time, I lay in bed as one paralyzed for I could not move a single muscle. I screamed for help but no sound managed to escape my lips so I just lay there, struggling desperately to wake from this horrifying attack. At long last, I succeeded in opening my eyes, thus ending the torment I was enduring. Upon awakening, I felt a precise pain on the surface of my stomach where the fiend had scratched with its claws. It was not until I fell asleep again that I was relieved of such pain entirely."

"How very curious," remarked Lord Kessler.

"Yes, I suppose," said Iara and observed that his visage had, for a moment or so it seemed, taken on a strange pallor. "There is a grand painting hanging above the mantel in the main drawing room," she continued, "It is a very impressive piece and of remarkable craftsmanship and artistry. I cannot help but gaze at it whenever I pass by."

"What were your thoughts upon seeing this painting?" asked the gentleman.

Iara replied, "I confess upon first seeing it, I was overcome with mild curiosity and enquired of Mrs. Harcourt the identity of the gentleman standing beside you. She answered only vaguely and told me that he was your dearest friend and that a tragedy had resulted in his demise and consequently, in your unending grief."

"Mrs. Harcourt is a dear lady but she speaks hastily at times," Lord Kessler said, "I have instructed her not to speak of this painting to anyone for it regards a matter I have long wished to forget."

"Forgive me for having alluded to this aspect of your past," said Iara, "Only the spirit of inquiry and regard for you moved me to ask of it."

Lord Kessler said, "Do not apologize. I appreciate your solicitude and understand your curiosity. The gentleman in the portrait with me was not only the most able soldier in my regiment but also my most cherished friend on this earth. His Imperial Majesty had the piece executed in our honor and presented as homage to our victory in Prague. When I left the court, I took this painting with me as a souvenir of my time there. It is a piece that is very precious to me because of the memories it holds."

"I am sorry to hear of your loss," said Iara, "If you are so intent on repressing those tragic memories, why do you keep the painting in such a prominent place where all who pass, including yourself, can see it?"

"Because the gentleman standing with me is very dear to me and while I do not wish to look back on my grief, I cannot and will not allow myself to forget it either," answered Lord Kessler and smiled warmly at her.

A feeling of elation came over Iara, a sensation she knew too well when in his company. Life was sweet; if not then, now. Lord Kessler made it so. He aroused such strong passions within her, such passions she could not restrain but only yield to. She would surrender her whole being to him and honor him with the faithfulness of her heart. She wanted to devote herself wholeheartedly to this gentleman whose godhood she had created. She would lavish him with endless romances and speak infinite praises in his honor. Love was hers to give and his to receive. He would drown in an ocean of her love and she would give him the breath of life.

She looked over the horizon and watched twilight come upon the land. She wanted the red glow of the sun to last forever so that she could always see Lord Kessler exactly as he stood before her now. She wanted to study that pose for all time, to gaze upon his heavenliness until the stars faded from his eyes. Was it unnatural to view him through jeweled spectacles, to behold such character in the holiest of light? Yet how brightly does he shine in the dark? A darkness unknown to her... *Wicked, impudent thought! Lord Kessler is all good.*

VI

A Starless Night

*W*hen Lord Kessler and Iara had returned from their excursion, they were greeted by Mrs. Ingram who told them, "Miss Lukas has just sent word of her arrival tomorrow afternoon."

"Tomorrow afternoon!" exclaimed Lord Kessler, "Why? Are we not to expect her in September?"

Mrs. Ingram shrugged. "A sudden change in schedule, I suppose," she replied.

"How very like her to just change things at a moment's notice," he uttered under his breath. He sighed and after Mrs. Ingram had left the room, said to Iara, "Miss Lukas is the daughter of one of my governesses when I lived in Austria. We became quite attached to each other and over time saw our friendship blossom into a passionate romance. Our courtship was not to last, however, for I resigned from my duties shortly after my campaign in Vienna and have never returned to court or to Austria since. Miss Lukas has been visiting me intermittently over the past year or two and we have both been heartened by such reunion.

"Her last visit, however, gave me cause to turn from her for she had informed me that she was engaged to the Marquis of Lienz, a nobleman whose estate was larger than mine. She entreated me to be compassionate towards her and further enjoined me to dismiss any sentiments I still had for her. I was solemnly hurt by the announcement of her engagement and the manner in which she had conveyed the news to me but I accepted it with equanimity and gave her my full blessing. Thenceforth, I resolved to disenthrall myself from any heart-ache that attended such loss and prayed earnestly for forbear-ance during those trying times and before long, my feelings towards Miss Lukas gradually faded until I no longer bore any amorous feelings for her."

He thought for a moment then said, "Miss Suri, I must ask you not to let my past involvement with Miss Lukas cloud your judgment of her for she has not yet given you any reason to dislike her."

"I will do as you say," Iara responded, "But even so, the slightest ignorance on her part will give me an excuse to think poorly of her. I cannot help it for I have determined to show you compassion as my affection for you forbids me to do otherwise."

Lord Kessler smiled and said, "As you wish, ma'am."

*L*ieutenant Vidur sat at the edge of the bed, his face buried in his hands. Iara sat down beside him and laid her head on his shoulder. He lifted his face and kissed her hair affectionately. She traced her finger over the tattoo spanning the length of his arm. There was a somber note in its design, the story of an empire woven into the tapestry of its history. She had an immense respect for him, for the allegiance he so dutifully upheld in serving the court and for the love he so graciously bestowed upon her. And in response to such virtue, she allowed her spirit to acknowledge in the most heartfelt manner her profound appreciation and esteem for the gentleman.

The essence of their romance lay in the passion they shared and in the faithfulness of their hearts. In a world that belonged not only to them, Lieutenant Vidur and Iara oftentimes found themselves the focal point of much discussion and as a fair contrast, the subject of much gossip. With respect to the former, there was always a specific element discussed which rendered praise – the exquisite grace and comeliness of Miss Suri, for instance, or the unsurpassable charisma of Lieutenant Vidur. With respect to the latter, however, points of interest were generally dissimilar on various levels. There was no doubt as to the affection shared between the two young lovers but, as is the case with gossip, such affection could only turn for the worst. It was the case, therefore, that word began to spread concerning the steadfastness of the pair's love. The lieutenant was habitually away in pursuit of heroic duties and errands, defending the nation from foreign invaders and other such threats. How frequently his visits were remained a mystery though, for his travels were spontaneous and like a bandit, he almost always stealthily crept away in the dark of the night, under the shade of the moon, and in no one's sight. There was absolutely nothing singular, therefore, about this particular night in which Iara's dream occurred.

A carriage had been seen making its way to Hayden Court in the middle of some starless night. From the carriage alighted a gentleman clothed in military attire. He came to a halt upon reaching the door. He stopped merely to allow a moment of disquiet to escape his mind so that a gentle tear could fall from his eye. The tear fell, a sigh came, then the bell was rung. A servant came to the door and let him into the house whereupon he proceeded posthaste to the chamber of his beloved.

"Sadhil, my darling!" exclaimed Iara, "What a pleasant surprise this is. I did not expect to see you tonight."

"I did not expect to come," said Lieutenant Vidur, "How I've missed you, dearest!"

Iara rushed to embrace him as was her wont and lavished him with her usual terms of endearment. He, in turn, lavished upon her plenty of kisses and other acts of adoration. Once the salutations had been pronounced and the romantic gestures relished, she sat down and waited for him to speak but he remained silent, fully absorbed in his own thoughts. He stood before her, his arms folded luxuriantly as he leaned against the wall. Even in this simple pose, there was a certain charm in him that she could not resist. She looked up at him, her eyes questioning the apparent distress on his face. He glanced at her, offered a halfhearted but sincere smile, then looked away. She found the whole rather disconcerting and implored him to reveal the source of his anguish.

"Sweetheart," he said, "I have not the words with which to relate this matter to you so that you will find even a bit of consolation in the message. In truth, I have slaved in earnest to find the right words but all my efforts have proved to no avail, hence you must forgive me and permit me to speak words that would give you cause to grieve."

The smile slowly faded from Iara's face as she pondered the meaning of his words. "Why do you keep me in suspense, my love?" she asked.

At this, Lieutenant Vidur no longer attempted to conceal the source of his despair and spoke with the greatest of care lest he should utter words which would cause her distress.

"I have been called to duty and must leave at once."

"How long shall you be gone?"

"I have been called to duty yet it is not this that brings

such heaviness upon my heart," said he, "My dear Iara, I have been called away this time to carry out a special mission, a mission that opposes the very principles I hold dear. As you may recall, I was summoned to court a few months ago to convene with Lord Rosenthal along with several others of my regiment. Our council took place under the shade of night and in the space of some forgotten dungeon. Lord Rosenthal informed us of a conspiracy that was growing increasingly powerful even as we spoke, one that demanded immediate suppression. According to His Lordship, evidence had been secretly gathered against the nine conspirators which verified their intent to depose the monarchy. Swift action is required on our part to protect His Majesty and to bring justice to those that threaten the security of his throne. I have been called upon to aid in crushing the conspirators before they can be given an opportunity to strike. The nature of this mission must never be made known outside our circle and the origin of this mandate to be revealed under no circumstance. I am telling you all this in the strictest of confidence."

"When shall you depart?" asked Iara.

"This night, even at this very moment," replied Lieutenant Vidur as he clasped her to his bosom, "I shall return to you soon, my love. We shall be together again as we are now, I promise you this."

VII

Affairs of the Heart

Miss Lukas strutted into the entrance hall, a sultry smile carved upon her luscious lips. Her beauty and glamour shone lustrously through the silky, flawless skin that covered her and the fashionable apparel she sported added even more opulence to her appearance. Every part of her person had been given great consideration, so much so that one would not be able to glimpse a single imperfection in any part she flaunted. A sense of unease lingered in Iara's mind; it was not so much the feeling of jealousy but rather, the fear of losing that aspect of Lord Kessler's attention and devotion she treasured so much.

"My dear Lord Kessler, how I've missed you!" exclaimed Miss Lukas.

"I trust that your journey here has been a pleasant one and that you are in the best of health, my lady," returned the gentleman.

After the necessary formalities had been made, Miss

Lukas turned to Iara and said, "I understand that you too have just arrived here, Miss Suri. I hope that my visit will not intrude on your time here."

"Not at all, Miss Lukas," Iara replied, "I am quite fond of making new acquaintances."

Miss Lukas smiled. "I shall keep your words in mind, my dear friend, and eagerly anticipate the pleasure of your company," said she.

Following their midday repast, the ladies gathered for tea in the drawing room while the gentlemen repaired to the library to indulge in a drink and discuss their usual politics behind locked doors. A generous assortment of freshly baked cakes, pastries, jellies, creams, and other sweet delicacies was arrayed neatly on the buffet table. Iara was just about to bite into a delicious slice of black forest cake when Miss Lukas approached her and requested the pleasure of her company to which she obliged, though only halfheartedly.

"Miss Suri, how do you like Schloss Valkuriz?" asked Miss Lukas.

"I like it very much indeed," answered Iara, "I cannot imagine a lovelier or more inviting place."

"Neither can I. I always enjoy coming here. It gives me a chance to visit England and to see Lord Kessler, of course. Such visit is my only solace, really. Have you been acquainted with the gentleman long?"

"No, we met only a few weeks ago."

"Is that so? I find it rather astonishing he would invite anyone to his castle after only such a brief acquaintance. I wonder his reason for doing so."

"The same I have for accepting his gracious request – I am fond of his society as he is fond of mine."

"How lovely," remarked Miss Lukas, "He is very much favored among the ladies, you know. I am sure you have your reason for visiting him." She paused briefly before continuing, "It's strange but I feel as if I must make a stronger effort to connect with you on account of my involvement with Lord Kessler in the past."

"Miss Lukas, you are not obligated to justify yourself to me. What happened between the both of you is really not my concern. Besides, I have no right to interfere in the matter."

"And yet I am forced to think myself culpable," said Miss Lukas, "I am quite certain he has spoken to you of me."

"He has mentioned you, yes. I believe he is the most compassionate of men and as such, harbors no resentment against those who have mistreated him in any way."

"Tell me, are you engaged to Lord Kessler?"

"I am not," Iara replied. Determined to disclose as little information as possible regarding her relationship with Lord Kessler, she displayed an air of mock concern and secretly vowed to answer each of Miss Lukas' subsequent questions with a mere word or two. Scarcely had the latter began interrogating her than she found herself breaking the oath she had just made.

"Do you not find him a most handsome gentleman?" asked Miss Lukas.

"Indeed, he is very handsome."

"Forgive me for being so inquisitive but has Lord Kessler ever expressed any interest in you?"

"He complimented me on my dancing," said Iara, "Does that signify interest?"

An awkward silence ensued in which Iara found herself absorbed in the intricate details of a statuette standing on the table, a marble replica of the *Augustus of Prima Porta*. She smiled to herself as she likened the image of Mr. Bradford to that of the statuette. There was Mr. Bradford posing in the traditional controposto manner with his right arm stretched out and his left leg slightly bent.

"I apologize for all these questions," Miss Lukas said, breaking the silence between them, "It's just that you possess a particular appeal that might entice such a man as Lord Kessler even if your standing is, shall we say, below his."

"Miss Lukas," said Iara, wandering back reluctantly to the conversation, "Should I not be the one to worry considering your past intimacy with the gentleman?"

"Perhaps," replied Miss Lukas, "Had our relationship not ended as it did, I would have believed your concern to be legitimate. But given the resentment he now bears towards me, what reason do you have to worry?" She took Iara's hand in hers and pressed it gently. "I have wronged him," said she, "I have destroyed a most precious romance and am suffering for it through my own remorse and through the discontent of my relationship with the Marquis. Miss Suri, I beseech you to entreat Lord Kessler on my behalf. Apprise him of the affection I nurtured for him in the past and the sincere love I still nurse for him."

"You cannot ask me even for a moment to endeavor to steer his heart in your direction," said Iara, "I wish not to play a part in influencing the feelings of so kind a gentleman."

"So my suspicion is true. You refuse to help me because you have fallen for him."

Iara immediately withdrew her hand and said, "Miss Lukas, pray do not presume to know my heart. My sentiments towards Lord Kessler should be no concern of yours for I have not displayed them so explicitly in your presence and even if I did and they prove to be as you say, I have not the slightest inclination to betray my heart."

"That is fair," Miss Lukas stated, "It is never easy for a lady to disregard her own feelings for the sake of another."

At that moment, the gentlemen stepped into the room to join their female companions.

"What are you two lovely ladies discussing so seriously over there?" Mr. Vartan enquired.

"We were simply discussing the convolutions of a fairly twisted world," answered Iara, delighted to be called away from her present situation, "Shall I play for you, sir?"

"Please, Miss Suri, it is always a pleasure to hear you play," said Mr. Vartan.

Lord Kessler walked over to the pianoforte and leaned over the instrument, watching her fingers as they danced across the keys.

"Miss Lukas is very beautiful," she said, looking up at him, "You forgot to tell me how beautiful she is."

He laughed. "It was a minor detail I deemed irrelevant, really," said he.

"Then let us speak no more of this," she said as her eyes returned to the song sheet and her mind to the music that surrounded her.

VIII

Pleasure and Pain

Upon entering the grand ballroom, the residents of Schloss Valkuriz handed in their cards and their names were duly announced, their status at once established, and the necessary formalities and introductions made. Lord Kessler, being the most distinguished gentleman in attendance, was given the honor of escorting the hostess to dinner. Iara, though saddened by this, found her discontent mildly increased by her being matched with Mr. Bradford who, upon seeing Lord Kessler paired with the hostess, immediately took the opportunity to conduct Iara to her place at the table. When every gentleman had escorted his assigned partner to dinner and every lady was comfortably seated, the grand ceremony of the dinner took place. After the banquet, all the guests rose from their seats to prepare for the dance.

The dance, being the single most anticipated event of the occasion, generated great excitement among the attendees and Iara was more than thrilled to share her first dance of the evening with Lord Kessler. Every eye turned in their direction as they waltzed. How ravishing a pair they looked on the dancefloor – Lord Kessler exquisitely arrayed in full evening attire and Iara resplendent in her elegant gown of ivory satin worn underneath a white sarsnet dress lavishly trimmed with diamantine lace.

After they had engaged in two consecutive dances, they were approached by Mr. Bradford. "Lord Kessler," said he, "I hope you don't intend to keep this fine young lady to yourself all night. May I?"

"Of course, if it pleases Miss Suri," replied Lord Kessler.

Mr. Bradford, having chosen Iara as a worthy partner on account of her brilliant execution of the quadrille with Lord Kessler, bestowed on her the honor of dancing the next two dances with him. Iara, having had absolutely no intention of earning such merit and having preferred to make a much less favorable impression on the gentleman had she been cognizant of his watchful eye, would certainly have purposefully performed some incorrect steps. In truth, the contempt she felt towards Mr. Bradford would not have been so strong had she not been so infatuated with Lord Kessler and she therefore not only found it impossible to spare even an ounce of adoration for another gentleman but also resented those who had the audacity to intrude on her feelings, feelings which were reserved only for Lord Kessler. As such, her disdain for Mr. Bradford was significantly and justifiably magnified in turn. And having no success in quickly declining his offer with a reasonable excuse, she was forced to give her assent. Accordingly, she found herself taking her place in the set and facing Mr. Bradford on the dancefloor.

"Miss Suri," said the gentleman as the dance commenced, the flicker of a smile upon his face, "Shall you make me wait in vain for the musical treat you promised me?"

"It has hardly been two days, sir," replied Iara, "Are you so impatient as to wait a little longer? I assure you, good things are worth waiting for."

"I confess, patience is not one of my strongest qualities, especially in matters concerning the heart."

"Such matters are oftentimes delayed when one fails to exercise virtue."

"Will you grant me that chance? Will you permit me to get to know you better in hopes of winning your affection?"

"You may do as you wish but I advise you that any such effort will prove futile."

"How so?"

"My affection is presently reserved for another."

"Do you mean Lord Kessler?"

"You are rather bold, sir, in asking that."

"Yes, that is my style. So what is it then? Do you love the man or not?"

"Mr. Bradford, we have not been acquainted with each other long enough for you to ask me such a question. It is enough for you at present to know that any effort on your part to pursue my affection shall prove futile."

The gentleman replied, "You can't mean that. With the deepest respect, I opened my heart to you yet you show no consideration whatsoever for my feelings. Are you so sure of yourself that you wish not to know my affection?"

"I meant no offense but my feelings towards you are unchanged and shall remain so for as long as we both shall live."

"You are quite an insolent young lady."

"I am merely being honest, sir," said she.

Scarcely impressed by her response, he declared in a hostile tone, "I assure you, ma'am, nothing escapes me. Everything I want is within my grasp. Everything!"

Seizing Iara by the hand, he tilted her suddenly to one side and then to the next, all the while concealing this act from the eyes of the public. His behavior convinced her to be less merciful in her judgment of his character in the future for he did not possess the gentle and modest attributes she found so attractive in the opposite sex. Instead, she found him to be a contemptible and vile man unworthy of her acquaintance and was determined to interact with him no longer until she felt him sufficiently punished for his absolute lack of civility.

Mr. Bradford, in turn, was affronted by the liberty with which she had taken in throwing her insults at him and convinced himself falsely that he regretted inviting her to dance or ever looking in her direction. His anger was appeased partly, however, by the manner of his dancing in which he could at least cause some amount of physical pain though her impertinent glances at him caused him displeasure. As social convention forbade Iara from removing herself from the floor before the dance was over, she was forced to remain dancing with Mr. Bradford until the music faded. At length, when the dance finally ended, she was greatly relieved and without another glance at her partner, quickly turned and walked away from him, leaving the proud and boastful gentleman to be further insulted.

"Are you having a good time, my dear?" Mrs. Ingram asked as Iara walked by.

"Yes, I'm delighted to be here."

"I am very glad to hear that. I dare say, there are some decent young men here who are in want of a dance partner. Shall I introduce you to a couple of them?"

"No, thank you, ma'am. I feel a little fatigued and need some air. Please excuse me."

"Of course, my dear," replied Mrs. Ingram, "You'll find the view from the balcony rather breathtaking."

Iara removed herself from the assembly hall and walked out into the balcony. As her thoughts turned to Lord Kessler, she felt a rage kindling inside of her. Why had he forsaken her and left her vulnerable to the attention and whims of Mr. Bradford? Why did he even permit that insufferable man to dance with her? Where was he when she needed him? She peered into the hall and saw Lord Kessler standing at the far side of the room conversing with his friends. Beside him was Miss Lukas, her hand resting on his arm and her eyes following his every movement. Miss Lukas suddenly turned and glanced in her direction. She bowed her head slightly to acknowledge Iara and smiled then looked away, her efforts at flirtation even more pronounced than before, the gestures carefully plotted so that they would in no way escape the observation of those around, especially Iara's.

Iara blushed with vexation and at once averted her eyes from the scene. How she despised it! Such vulgar conduct! Such crude portrayal of untamed desire! Every glance, every gesture made by Miss Lukas struck her as a venomous arrow of hate. Those devious eyes which screamed at her were fraught with malice and contempt, surreptitiously confirming the disdain that their owner felt for her and thus her own detestation of Miss Lukas.

The man I adore in the arms of that bitch! Lord Kessler, are you the gentleman I fancied you to be? Or are your wicked traits hidden behind that treacherous smile you wear so handsomely? So mysteriously...

IX

A Declaration of Love

"Miss Suri," Lord Kessler called from behind, "I must compliment you once again on the gracefulness of your dancing. You execute the steps of the quadrille exceptionally well, I must say. I was watching you as you danced with Mr. Bradford. Had he not asked you, I would have had the pleasure myself."

Iara did not respond nor did she turn to look at him. She was staring out at the night sky, gazing at the constellations that adorned the vast space above. She closed her eyes and felt her hair fluttering as the gentle breeze touched her face.

"Miss Suri, will you not give me an answer?" asked Lord Kessler as he walked up to her. But she remained silent. "You are not in good spirits," he remarked, "What is troubling you, my dear girl?"

"Nothing."

"Then speak to me."

"I have nothing to say to you, sir."

"What? No words?"

"None. You should go back before you are missed."

"Am I not missed here?"

"Should you be? And by whom, sir?" asked Iara, "By the gentleman who sits in that corner with his bottle of brandy or by the two ladies who stand gossiping over there?"

"Your words are cold tonight; they cut like ice," said Lord Kessler, "If I have wronged you in any way, let me know and I shall make amends for my behavior."

"You have not wronged me. I blame myself for all that I feel."

"And what is it that you feel?"

"At this moment, nothing," was her curt answer.

"What transgression was committed on my part to earn your displeasure this evening, ma'am?" he asked, "Tell me, have I committed a breach of protocol in your presence or in the presence of those around me? Have I comported myself in a fashion that was not to your liking?"

"No," replied Iara, "You have behaved most respectably as you have always done."

"We are good friends now and may speak to each other as we like," said the gentleman, "Therefore, I beseech you to be forthright with me."

"Then I shall tell you, sir. You let yourself be entranced by the charms of that sorceress. She is no friend of mine and in pleasing her, you displease me."

Lord Kessler replied, "My feelings towards Miss Lukas have been made known to you as is the assurance that any sentiments I bore for her in the past are no more. Therefore, this jealousy of yours is unfounded."

"How dare you accuse me of jealousy!" rejoined Iara, "What reason do I have to be jealous? Tell me, what reason is there?"

"Then why are you so upset?" he asked.

She answered, "Because it sickens me whenever I see you with her. The way she looks at you, it disgusts me!"

"Her eyes tell me nothing and mine say nothing to her," he declared, "If I have displeased you in any way, you have my sincerest apology. But don't expect me to give justification for a vice that is not mine. I don't appreciate being accused of such conduct by you or by anyone. I advise you to reconsider your assertions, ma'am. Search your heart for the truth."

"My heart? What heart is there to consult when what heart there is has been coldly received by the one that receives its affection?"

"Miss Suri –"

"I must go now, sir."

As Iara proceeded to leave, Lord Kessler grabbed her hand and gently pulled her back. He gazed into her eyes for a long time and still holding her, said softly, "You must never leave me, do you hear? Never, not even for a moment. I cannot bear to lose you."

"You cannot ask me to stay while you dance and consort with that harlot. You have no right!" said Iara.

"I have every right," declared he, "For your happiness is my concern and I refuse to let you go until I have restored such happiness in you."

"Such happiness is not mine to know; it belongs to Miss Lukas."

"She will have no such privilege. My affections are reserved for another lady."

"You have yet to convince me of that, sir, for I am aware of no such lady."

"Do you mean to tell me then that all my efforts thus far have been in vain?" he asked.

A moment of silence ensued as Iara turned from him in a desperate effort to conceal the tears that started to stream down her face. Lord Kessler pulled her gently towards him and clasped her in his arms.

"Don't hide your tears, Miss Suri. Hide nothing from me," he said as he wiped the tears from her eyes, "Do you worry that the affection I have for you is no more because Miss Lukas is here?" He laughed and said, "Silly girl, what reason have you to doubt my heart? Do you not see it is beating for you? When I separated with Miss Lukas, an intense grief had set upon me so that I did not think that I could appreciate life again. But that burden was quickly lifted when I saw your face that day at Hayden Court. How my heart sang when you spoke to me, when your eyes lit up to meet mine. I prayed I would see those beautiful eyes again and wrote to you because I longed for your companionship. Each moment I spend here with you is a blessing. You give meaning to my life and reason for me to endure. You are like an angel to me, so pure and precious. So is my love for you. You need not fear that it would falter even in the slightest way. If you care for me as I care for you, put your trust in me. Do you love me, Miss Suri? If you do, then profess your love to me and give me an honest declaration."

"I love you, Lord Kessler," said Iara, tears glistening in her eyes.

"Call me Nikolas."

"I love you, Nikolas," said she, "I love you as I love no other. My feelings for you need no proclamation. They are written in my eyes and on my lips and are strengthened within my heart and in my soul. I am yours and yours alone, forever and always."

The evening seemed almost surreal to Iara and she did not want it to end. The moon shone luminously in the sky, its crescent shape prominent against the dark of the night. She gazed at the starry jewels that decorated the night sky. In the dazzling moonlight, they glittered in every direction like diamonds in the dark.

Within an hour, they arrived at the castle and made their way directly towards Lord Kessler's chamber and once inside, they embraced in the soft effulgence of the candles. Slowly, he loosened her dress, revealing the silken flesh that lay beneath.

"What's the matter, Iara?" he asked as she trembled in his arms.

And she, already captive to his charms, said almost forcedly, "I can't. I'm sorry."

He held unto her dress for a while longer, his fingers entwined in the laces of her gown. Then slowly, very slowly, he released his grasp.

"You're not upset, are you?" she asked.

"Of course not," he replied, "You wish to maintain your chastity. I respect you for that." She smiled, comforted. He drew even closer to her so that his breath was warm upon her cheek and said, his voice suffused with passion, "And while I cannot relish the taste of your body, Iara, I can at least savor the taste of your lips."

X

A Brutal Assignment

*G*rant me forgiveness, my love, for I am to stain my hands with the blood of innocent men," Lieutenant Vidur said as he drew his sword and gazed at it. In the subdued glow of the candle, the cerulean diamonds sparkling on its hilt added a soft luster to its blade.

"You need not seek my forgiveness for you will always have it," said Iara, "I know your heart and I know the purity of your soul."

Lieutenant Vidur approached the window and tore open the curtains. For a while, he stood there, looking out thoughtfully, his hands pressed against the pane.

"I have slain countless men in battle and many more will I slay if His Majesty orders it," declared he, "For I kill these men with the grace of God and with my sovereign's blessing. But this new task that has been assigned to us forces us to execute even those that are innocent in the eyes of the world and who have not yet tasted blood... women and children.

Not only are we to murder these innocents in cold blood but also to commit these vicious crimes in the name of God."

"No!" cried Iara, getting up and hastening towards him, "Sadhil, you cannot do this. Please, I beg you."

"You condemn me?" he said, "I couldn't bear it if you –"

"I don't condemn you, dearest," she replied, "I only ask you to abandon this charge of yours."

"When I became a soldier of the court, I pledged an oath of allegiance to the king and to his council, hence I must carry out this assignment as commanded. More importantly, I cannot forsake my comrades who suffer with me in this ordeal for they are no less burdened by this than I am."

Iara rested her head on his shoulder. "Then may God have mercy on your soul and reward you for your dedication in serving the court," she said.

"And yet do I deserve such mercy?" he said. He brought his hands before his eyes and staring at them, said, "These hands, once stained with the blood of innocents, cannot be washed clean again."

"I fear your virtue and integrity will be the cause of your destruction."

"If such is the case, I shall embrace martyrdom as if God demands it Himself."

"I shall be like a widow who tears at her own heart and spends her days staring at a barren earth that spits out fallen soldiers. Sadhil, my love, am I to see you among those men whose faces profess anguish and death? Tell me, darling, am I to wear my mourning gown when I hear your name pronounced again?"

"My darling Iara, I would rather have a thousand swords plunge into the depth of my heart than see you shed a single tear for my sake," Lieutenant Vidur said, folding her tightly in his arms, "There is nothing I desire more than to be by your side tonight and all nights hereafter but this accursed fate that has fallen on me prohibits me from fulfilling this desire of mine. It is thus with a heavy heart that I go from you this night to perform my duty. Do not worry about me, my sweet. God is good to me; He will preserve me throughout this ordeal." Then he kissed her passionately on the lips and assured her, "When the crescent moon is high in the sky and the stars smile down on you, know that I am near."

*T*he golden rays of the sun pierced the enormous glass windows, showering the chamber with luminescence. Lord Kessler's chamber was the most magnificent of all the rooms within the castle walls. Furnished in rose gold, lending the place an ambience of sheer exquisiteness, the style of the chamber was reminiscent of the opulent rooms of contemporary Parisian chateaux. The glamorous silk curtains hanging around the elegant four-poster bed were finely embroidered with pearl rosettes that glistered in every direction. The walls all around were decorated with exuberant artwork featuring breathtaking landscapes and stunning imagery rendered in delicate shades. Iara took a turn about the room, admiring the many illustrations and reading their narratives.

A beautiful golden locket attached to a golden chain lay on the escritoire, inside of which was the portrait of a gentleman whose face bore the likeness of the soldier standing beside Lord Kessler in the painting above the mantelpiece. Who was he and what secrets did he hold? What mystery was enclosed in this very locket?

"Lady Weston was quite a scandalous picture at the ball, was she not?" Miss Preston said at breakfast. She winked at Mr. Vartan. "I dare say, she suited your taste quite perfectly."

Mr. Vartan scoffed gently at the statement and asked, "Do you really think that I would succumb to such licentious behavior?"

"Yes, I do," was Miss Preston's response.

"Well then, you are right," declared the gentleman, "No matter, such women as Lady Weston are intended only for the more abandoned pleasures of life. In any case, I was not the only one amusing myself last night. My dear friend here left the party early and not without a cheerful heart too."

"Ah yes, he and Miss Suri were not with us on the journey home," Mrs. Ingram remarked, smiling, "I wondered where they went."

"Perhaps they needed some fresh air," Mr. Ingram joined

in, having finished the last morsel of food on his plate and beckoning to one of the servants to refill his cup.

"There is really nothing to suspect," Lord Kessler said, "I grew weary of the soirée and persuaded Miss Suri to run away with me." He winked at Iara as he took a bite of his toast, then turning to Mr. Vartan, said, "With so many pretty damsels in your corner, Alexander, I'm surprised you had time even to notice my leaving."

Mr. Vartan replied, "I am never too engaged to notice my dear friends. Even if I should dance with Aphrodite herself, I should still think of you, Nikolas."

"Yes, so should we all," declared Miss Lukas, then remarked, "How lovely."

"What, my dear?" asked Mrs. Ingram.

"Why, the flowers Mr. Bradford sent Miss Suri, of course," she replied, directing their attention to a bouquet of flowers standing on the far table, "They were delivered yesterday while Miss Suri was out." She smiled at Iara and added, "To be singled out by Mr. Bradford, how delightful indeed!"

All eyes turned towards the bouquet – all eyes except Iara's for hers were on Lord Kessler who only looked up momentarily from his plate to glance at Iara whose face was suffused with color. She opened her mouth to speak but no words managed to escape her lips. He looked away and continued eating in silence.

XI

A Dark Secret

As Iara stepped into the hall, she saw Lord Kessler standing by the door, dressed in full riding attire.

"Nikolas!" she called out. He turned around and looked at her in amusement as she rushed towards him.

"Dear girl, what on earth would possess a lady of your station to run across the hall like that?" he asked when they stood beside each other.

She took a moment to catch her breath, then said, "About the flowers, I care nothing for them. They're just –"

At this the gentleman laughed – a most welcome interruption indeed, thought she. "Neither do I," he said, smiling, "I already know your loyalties lie with me."

"Yes," said Iara, "Yes, of course." She stood there and watched as Lord Kessler mounted his horse and sped off across the field. It was a very delightful spectacle for her, especially now that her mind had been relieved of its burden and was consequently at liberty once more to indulge in the delights of the day.

She was soon joined by Miss Lukas who said, "I wonder, Miss Suri, if you would be so kind as to take a turn with me about the garden," and before a proper reply could be given, locked her elbow around Iara's and began walking with her.

The first part of their stroll was marked by polite laughter and occasional utterances of a very casual nature – a general comment on the weather perhaps or a newly formed opinion on one of the many guests at the ball the previous evening. Such parameters of conversation were keenly observed by both as they watched Lord Kessler gallop across the meadow while entertaining his audience with daring feats of gallantry on the stallion whereupon they showered upon him due compliments and applause.

"He's not wholly innocent, you know," said Miss Lukas.

"Lord Kessler is the quintessence of virtue to me," Iara said in return.

"Such a man as he may seem the quintessence of virtue but I can assure you he has his own dark secrets."

"Everyone has secrets they wish to keep and Lord Kessler is entitled to his own. He has been through so much. I find his courage and perseverance truly inspiring."

"Courage and perseverance?" laughed Miss Lukas, "In what, pray tell? Had you but the slightest idea –"

"Look, here he comes now!" exclaimed Iara, waving to Lord Kessler who, having ridden much to his contentment and delight, was now ambling towards them, reins in hand.

"Ladies," he greeted them, his face glowing from his recent exercise.

"You were the subject of our conversation just now," Miss Lukas told him.

"Was I? Well, I'm very thrilled to hear that," said the gentleman, "Though I should perhaps take my leave now. I would not wish to interrupt such a conversation between you two. Kindly excuse me."

Miss Lukas at once grabbed him by the arm and cried, "No, do stay!"

Her lack of decorum took him quite by surprise and he responded, much to her dissatisfaction, "You'll forgive me, ma'am."

She withdrew her hand upon realizing her error and now spoke with a greater degree of propriety, "We should both like you to stay, sir." And turning to Iara, she added, "Is that not so, Miss Suri?" to which Lord Kessler also turned towards Iara and she towards him so that their eyes were locked in each other's gaze.

Iara answered, "Yes, I should like that very much."

He smiled warmly at her and said, still looking fixedly into her eyes, "Then I shall have to oblige."

A flush of color rose in Miss Lukas' cheeks. "And why is that, sir?" she demanded.

"Why is what?" he asked, turning slowly towards her, his

gaze having been broken by that familiar voice.

When the question received no answer, he made no attempt to enquire further and started towards the castle, the women following at a full stride's length behind him. They walked in silence for some time before the seed of jealousy which had already taken root in Miss Lukas' heart began to blossom.

"The Marquis sends his regards," said she.

"Please convey to him my kind regards," he returned.

Another wave of silence passed among them. Miss Lukas, seeing that her arrow of spite had missed its mark and that the shot had produced a degree of hurt far less than she had anticipated, began to devise in that cold and calculating mind of hers a new plan of attack.

"Miss Suri thinks you are the quintessence of virtue," she said, "Is that not so, Miss Suri?"

"Miss Lukas, please," replied Iara, her eyes fixed on Lord Kessler who only glanced cursorily in their direction.

Miss Lukas laughed loudly. "The quintessence of virtue, indeed!" she said, assuming the same self-satisfactory and triumphant air, "You know, during our courtship, there was one to whom he was more devoted than he was to me. I could always tell when he had returned from seeing her."

"Please," begged Iara.

But Miss Lukas would not relent. "There was always a kind of glow in his face, like an ecstatic renewal of faith," she continued, "It was very frustrating for me and whenever I questioned him about his fidelity, he always assured me that there was no other woman in his heart except me."

"He may have behaved suspiciously but I am convinced he had cause to do so and whatever cause he had was noble," Iara said, "Pray don't judge him without first having sufficient knowledge of his circumstances." These words were spoken rather hastily in his defense in a desperate attempt to dismiss the issue entirely.

Miss Lukas shrugged. "It was not just this that troubled me. Shortly after his campaign in Vienna, he resigned from the court and declared that he would never return to Austria again." Here she paused and cast a furtive glance at the gentleman from underneath the brim of her hat.

Iara glanced at Lord Kessler, hoping she would not find his countenance disturbed and in this she was disappointed. The muscles in his jaws tightened and she detected a rising indignation in him, concealed by the collectedness of his features, though how long and in what capacity he would be able to maintain such composure, she knew not.

Miss Lukas was fully aware of the anguish her words had provoked yet this was invitation enough to carry on.

"He did not tell me the reason for his sudden resignation and departure from the court," she continued, "Something had transpired while he was away, you see, something totally beyond his control. I am sure of it."

Lord Kessler, who had remained gracefully complaisant throughout all this, at length turned around and spoke.

"That's enough, madam. I beg you to withhold your assertions."

Still she would not yield. "I dared not inquire into the matter for fear of incurring his wrath. He has never talked about it since," she said and moved closer towards him, her eyes fixed on his, "It was very strange. It's like he's hiding a dark secret from the world."

"I said that's enough!" said the gentleman.

"What did you do in Austria, sir?" she demanded, glowering at him, "What heinous crimes did you commit at court? Why did you run off the way you did? What was it you were trying to escape?"

"Quiet!" shouted Lord Kessler.

"Never!" cried Miss Lukas, "Miss Suri should know the truth if she means to court you. She should know the villain you really are! You and that bloodthirsty Lieu–"

She could not finish this sentence, however, for he had raised his hand in anger and had slapped her so hard across the cheek that it instantly turned red. Miss Lukas lifted her hand to return the slap but he seized it, denying her the pleasure. She pulled away from him forcefully, tears pouring from her eyes. Seeing the servants staring at them in bewilderment, their tasks now forgotten, she cast her eyes on the ground in deep humiliation.

He drew near her and she looked up at him in fear. The fiery glare in his eyes, however, forced her to look away. He pressed his lips against her ear. "I dare you to utter another word," he said, his voice imbued with malice and contempt. She trembled and dared not look into his eyes.

"Prepare the carriage for Miss Lukas' departure!" he shouted to the servants, "Quickly!"

She turned to Iara, a silent plea upon her lips.

"You knew his temper," said Iara softly.

Miss Lukas stormed immediately towards the readied carriage. She threw one final glance at them before stepping inside, the expression on her face one of resignation for it was clear to them all, herself included, that she had lost. The door shut behind her and the carriage rolled away and disappeared through the gates.

Iara turned to Lord Kessler. "You were quite harsh on her, don't you think?" she said. He gave no reply and turning from her, walked briskly towards the schloss.

"Nikolas!" she called, hurrying after him, "Nikolas, wait!"

He turned around abruptly. Looking intently into her eyes, he said, his voice marked by the same coldness that had infused it earlier, "Miss Suri, you will address me properly in the presence of servants. Do you understand?"

She nodded in silence whereupon he turned and continued walking towards the castle.

XII

A Strange Message

*L*ord Kessler said to Iara when they were alone in the drawing room, "My exchange with Miss Lukas earlier this afternoon and the manner in which I dealt with her, it must have been quite a shock to you."

"Yes," replied Iara, "I confess I was very much surprised by her assertions and even more so by your reaction to them."

"And do you believe her assertions to be false?" he asked.

"Yes, of course," replied she.

"Do you really?"

"I want to, Nikolas."

"But you don't," he said. And when she gave no answer, he said, "It's not easy being a soldier in times of war, you know. The battlefield is but a graveyard, a meeting place for lost souls."

"And where was this battlefield?" she enquired.

He looked away, a melancholy expression in his eyes, and responded, his voice mellow and subdued, "Within."

"I understand," she said softly, resting her hand gently on his arm, "I'm sorry to have doubted you in any way. Say you'll forgive me." She knew that in questioning him, she had evoked hurtful memories within him, memories that he had long sought to repress, and so did not question him further though she found her fascination with him and curiosity in his past heightened as a result.

"Iara, I –"

Just then, a servant of the castle came into the room and following him was a boy of not yet fifteen years of age, the latter clutching a bottle of rum in his hand.

"What's this?" demanded Lord Kessler.

The servant explained that he had been drinking at the tavern just now as his work schedule enabled him to spend the rest of the day making merry outside the grounds of the castle. Whilst there, a fight broke out between the young man now presented before his master and another man at the tavern, which did not disturb him in the least since such violent incidents as this were commonplace in taverns. However, when the boy uttered a peculiar remark pertaining to a certain Lady Thorne – he could not recall what he had said due to the absurd nature of the statement – it caught his attention and he immediately turned to the ongoing fight whereupon he recognized the boy at once and knew him to be Darien. Darien had indulged to the point of intoxication and had in his state of drunkenness offended two men of ill repute, one of whom promptly assaulted him. Fortunately, the police arrived just in time to stop the fight before Darien suffered any major injury.

"Darien is my ward," Lord Kessler told Iara in an aside after the servant had been dismissed, "His father was a soldier in the royal army. His son was only six when he fell in battle and his wife in her eighth month of pregnancy. When she delivered a stillborn babe, she became so devastated that she suffered sporadic bouts of insanity and ultimately became very ill and died. Soon afterwards, Darien was adopted by a lieutenant in my regiment with whom he stayed for several years until he ran away at the age of thirteen. With scarcely any funds on his person, he lived on the streets for some time, living on the means of his meager purse. I happened upon him in the slums one day and took him home with me. Needless to say, his reckless and impudent ways, along with his sublime disregard for society, compelled me to eventually dismiss him from my castle."

Darien, having somewhat recovered from his insobriety, cast his eyes on the pair.

"What happened to you?" Lord Kessler asked.

"Is this the welcome I am to receive?" said the boy, "No sweet embrace or endearing terms, sir? Words of no consequence should not expect meaningful responses."

"Answer my question."

"And what question is that? I have quite forgotten."

"Do not play the fool with me, Darien."

"I needed to escape from this earthly prison that surrounds me. It is dark and dreary and filled with the demons of the netherworld," Darien replied.

"It is a hell for you only because you made it so yourself," rejoined Lord Kessler.

"You're right. I fashioned my own heaven and hell and while hell does not grant me satisfaction, heaven does," Darien said, holding up the bottle of rum in his hand, "Only rum has the power to bring me happiness, even if such happiness is only transient in nature. Why, you, of course, do not need to befriend this bottle of rum. You have no need to seek such happiness. I see it is already in your possession." He glanced at Iara as he said this.

"I will not tolerate such insolence!" shouted Lord Kessler as he stormed towards the boy, "You are a guest in my castle and while you are here, you will give me due respect!"

"Respect!" laughed Darien, "You are quite mistaken, sir. I am not Lieutenant Vidur. You cannot solicit respect from me by merely –"

Lord Kessler's countenance flushed with rage. At once he snatched the bottle of rum and smashed it so hard against the wall that a shard of glass brushed past the boy's cheek, leaving a fresh bruise upon his face.

"I should thank you, miss," said Darien, turning to Iara, "Were it not for your presence, Lord Kessler would have beaten me senseless."

"That's not true," said Iara and glanced at Lord Kessler whose mien conveyed to her that there was admittedly some truth in what was said as it expressed no denial of such accusation.

"Lady Thorne," Darien said, turning back to Lord Kessler.

At this Lord Kessler's visage instantly took on a frightful pallor, a strange bleakness that Iara had only once observed in him and at that time feared to see again.

"What of her?" he enquired.

"She's no longer a ghost in our world," answered Darien.

"What did you say?" asked Lord Kessler.

When the statement was repeated, albeit reluctantly by the speaker, he stepped back from the boy, utterly speechless. And without a word, he sat down on the sofa, his face turned away from them in deep contemplation.

XIII

Shadows of the Past

*Y*ou must think me a rogue, miss," said Darien, "I confess I know nothing of social graces or savoir faire. And I shan't endeavor to humor anyone with such affectations in order to prove myself respectable either."

"What has brought such gloom upon your world?" asked Iara.

"Trials and tribulations are foreign to you and Lord Kessler because you foolishly live your lives in dreams and fantasies," he replied, "I am only fourteen but I have seen enough calamity in this world to know that happiness is a false notion for the oppressed."

"Is that why you drink all the time? So you can drown your sorrows?"

He grew silent and for a while she could not discern the expression on his face.

"Who is this Lady Thorne of whom you spoke just now?" she asked.

"That's not her real name," said Darien, "It's what I call her – quite fitting, I suppose. Lord Kessler knows her by another name, her real name."

"And what name is that?"

"I don't know," the boy answered, "And even if I did, I'd rather not say."

"Who is she?"

"A twisted snake in the grass, that's what she is," he replied, clenching his fists, "A treacherous femme fatale with a stone-cold heart."

"Surely you don't mean that," said Iara.

"I do," he retorted, "I was only a young boy when I was placed under the care of Lady Thorne. I was not more than nine at the time but I knew hate. I knew it in my heart for there she had planted its seed and I kept it in the very depth of my soul even for many years to come. And out of that seed of hatred stemmed dark and painful memories and I nurtured its fruits for the length of my youth. And in those years, I learned fear and the consequences of such emotion for that lesson was constantly forced upon me.

"In those days, the lieutenant reigned; his word was law and suffice it to say, Lady Thorne adhered to his rule. In time, however, the black void in her was filled with bitter arrogance which eventually culminated in unholy vengeance and with devious intent, she crafted the wicked designs that drew the lieutenant's last breath. The circumstances surrounding his death are suspicious. Some claim he was poisoned by the sadistic cruelties of war that only those present can witness and found refuge at the point of his sword. Others contend he was assassinated, killed during a mutinous rage. These are just rumors, stories concocted to satisfy the populace. It is easier than you think for one cannot find evidence to prove otherwise. But I know the truth of the matter. I know what came to pass that night for I have seen the shape of Lady Thorne's heart and the face of the monster who murdered the good lieutenant."

He paused for a moment and closed his eyes tightly, as if trying to physically push the remembrance from his mind. "I see that bitch every hour of my waking life and at night she haunts my dreams like a crimson ghost," he said and opened his eyes once more, "And it seems no matter what I do, I can't escape her. That is why I drink."

They both fell silent for a while.

"Will you be joining us for dinner?" asked Iara.

Darien's eyes widened in astonishment. "Joining you for dinner?"

"Yes," said Iara, regarding him with the same measure of astonishment, "Do you not eat dinner or do you keep town hours?"

"But I don't belong to your world," said the boy, "Look at me. Can't you see I'm not one of you?"

"That's of no consequence," she responded, "It's what

resides on the inside that counts, isn't it? After all, you're Lord Kessler's ward. You are family, aren't you?"

He stared at Iara. Her words had greatly astounded him. She perceived that his physiognomy had altered considerably, almost instantaneously it seemed. It grew softer now and the stark reserve that had defined it earlier now disappeared almost completely.

"I can see you're not like the others," he said, "You treat me with respect. Forgive me for having judged you wrongly. I hope our paths shall cross again." He bowed politely, cast a final glance at her, then left the room.

"Nikolas," said Iara, hastening towards Lord Kessler.

He was staring vacantly before him, his eyes glassy. She touched him on the shoulder. He turned suddenly towards her as if stirred from a trance and said, "I am well, Iara," and glancing behind him, asked, "Is he gone?"

She nodded. "He spoke to me of Lady Thorne," she said and hoped he would satisfy her with more information on this mysterious damsel.

But her thirst for such knowledge remained unsatiated for he told her plainly, "Forget what he told you. The boy speaks nonsense." Then he rose from the sofa and took her hand. "Come with me," he said.

They made their way towards the east wing of the castle and entered the oriental drawing room, a magnificently furnished room boasting classic art and architecture reminiscent of ancient Chinese culture.

"This place is very special to me," Lord Kessler said, "Here I am offered the perfect solace when I have need of quiet meditation or silent prayer. When I'm here, I am able to obtain peace and equilibrium amid the chaos of this world and I thank God for giving me the strength to endure such harsh realities."

"Are you so consumed with grief that you cannot see the treasures you possess?" said Iara, "Many people would think that you have the world, Nikolas. And far many more would die to have a share of that world, to live even a moment as you live."

"Yes, so they would. But those who envy me would likewise find reason to pity me," said Lord Kessler, "I confess that in my youth, I placed the pursuit of wealth and honor above my Christian duties. It wasn't until I had lost the one dearest to my heart that I began to see past the pettiness of such secular pursuits and open my heart to what truly mattered, acknowledging Christ as my Savior and knowing Him. These treasures of which you speak are mere illusions to me. Underneath this facade of wealth and nobility lies a poor, wretched man who yearns desperately for a glimpse of Heaven."

"Do you not feel that you have accomplished something meaningful in this lifetime?"

"I can attest to the virtue of love," he answered. He

looked at her for a moment, a glimmer of despair washed over his countenance, then put down his wine glass and went over to the fireplace. He took the poker standing by the grate and poked casually at the lumps of coal burning inside. The flames rose, adorning the hearth with their fiery dance.

"I once loved a man who was worth all the love I gave him and more," he said, gazing into the fire, "A true friend he was to me, a fellow soldier who taught me the importance of sacrifice and the duty of brotherhood. He showed me the beauty of the world when my eyes were closed and imparted to me the truth of life when my faith became weak. He was my rock in times of distress and I became the rack on which he lay. Time is not the healer of grave wounds, Iara. One cannot be truly healed until one attains assurance that happiness is within one's reach. My happiness is secured in the conviction that someday, I shall be reunited with him when we meet again in that blissful place that awaits us."

A moment of silence passed. Iara could hear the fire crackling in the hearth as the flames rose higher and higher. In the luminosity of the fire, she discerned in his eyes a deep sadness and it disheartened her to see him like that.

"Nikolas –"

"My heart yearns for him still," he continued, "The remembrance of our past continues to haunt me. Even in sleep, his spirit moves within me and speaks to me, reassuring me of his steadfast friendship."

Iara touched him on the shoulder. He turned around.

"Forgive me, Iara. I should not have aroused such emotions in myself. I only hope that your opinion of me will always remain as it is now."

Iara smiled reassuringly. "Nikolas, if my opinion of you does change, it shall only be for the better. Knowing what I know now about the sadness you carry in your heart, I have even more reason to sympathize with you. How daunting it must have been for you to carry this heavy burden on your own! Was there no one with whom you shared your grief?"

He answered, "Only Mrs. Harcourt is cognizant of my pain. In my distress, I divulged everything to her." Then he smiled warmly at her and said, "We have been truly blessed, you and I, for we have both found the very joy we sought all our lives, even if only to glimpse it for a fleeting moment, and such profound joy it is, to be so favored among men. Have faith, Iara! The love our Father has for us cannot be surpassed nor can it be denied for He has proved it most faithfully through the blood of Jesus so that we may revel in His glory when we enter His divine kingdom. So you see, it is a far better fate that awaits us compared to the ephemeral happiness we experience on this earth."

XIV

Faded

The joys of the past in all their splendor had now turned into woes of the present and uncertainties of the future. The phantom shadows of the dark appeared, their forms lurking in the shade of night. And nestled among these shadows were two young lovers.

"Farewell, my love," said Lieutenant Vidur as he kissed Iara for the last time, "I shall return to you on a moonlit night when the heavens are graced with the beauty of the stars."

As the mist grew thicker and thicker against the solitude of the night, the memories that sprung in Iara's mind were gradually starting to lose their essence so that she knew only the cold of the mist and saw only the gloom that surrounded her. Lieutenant Vidur had come to her that night to deliver a tragic message, to impart somber words that offered no hope of reassurance. The details of his message eluded her mind; its fragments were like grains of sand lying on a strand, sailing with the wind on an endless journey, never to be touched again.

And in this desert of oblivion, she could not even recall the one who had conveyed the message. Who was he who had come to her just now? The moon glared at her amid the vast starless expanse. She touched her face and felt the wetness of her tears. Why were her eyes red and swollen with grief even at this hour? What could be the cause of such immense sorrow? Why had she gotten out of bed? Was it to receive a visitor? It could not be for who would call on her at such a late hour as this?

Something gleamed in the dark and she turned to look at the object. It was the rose, the mystical object that had only now surfaced in her consciousness. It glistered like a lost ruby in the dark, emanating an intense aura of crimson. In her eagerness to discover its mystery, she found herself drawing closer and closer to its compelling beauty as she made her way through the dark towards the place of luminosity. She examined the flower, surveying the crimson petals that secretly sheltered the memory of a lost love. The rose continued to glow and the mist continued to thicken until she was soon enfolded in a shroud of red and white.

Deep within her heart, Iara glimpsed her last embrace with Lieutenant Vidur. She closed her eyes and he was gone. Now he was gone again as she opened her eyes. But the tears were still there, the tears that had started on that fateful night and had not ceased since. How long had it been since then? It seemed like an eternity, an eternity without her lover. Yet the constant reminder provided by the rose seemed rather a painful confirmation of loss than a token of reassurance.

Sadhil, my love, I remember now. I remember everything. Where are you, my precious darling?

Something stirred her from her slumber, the dream perhaps. She turned towards the dressing table and saw lying on the vanity an ornate jewelry box. She opened the box to reveal a neatly folded velvet cloth. Wrapped inside the cloth was the rose. In the silvery light of the moon, it exuded a truly sinister appearance. So ghastly was its appearance that she shuddered at the sight.

Clothed with the veil of death, the once beautiful and enchanting rose had now become a terrifying sight to behold. The bright crimson that had given the flower its perennial beauty had now faded into a pale dullness. The petals were shriveled up and crushed and appeared to have suffocated in the casket it occupied. Torn and exposed as if condemned to an eternal quietus, the rose's edges curled inwards. The delicate head drooped down in self-pity, its wretched state highlighted by the dark lines that ran throughout the surface of the petals. The leaves, now golden brown in color and aged in appearance, were curled in a grotesque manner as though beckoning for the merciful hand of death itself.

$\mathcal{A}$ visage of solemnity dawned on Lord Kessler's face as he listened to Iara speak.

"What is this, Iara?" he asked as he opened the small casket and glimpsed the rose within, "What relevance does this hold?"

"That night, he came to me; he came to bring me grief," she said, "He wanted my forgiveness for the atrocious deeds he would commit – a mission he could not relate for he had sworn an oath of secrecy on pain of death. Before he departed, he promised that he would return to me and gave me this rose as a token of that promise. The faithfulness of the love I bear him is measured by the vitality of this rose. It has survived for so long because of my undying love for him which I had honored most faithfully as I had not given my heart to another man since. But when I made that declaration of love to you, I shattered its immortality and secured the path for its destruction."

Lord Kessler drank the last sip of champagne in his glass and said, "When you played that song at Hayden Court the first night we met, I sensed a haunting note in its melody and a tinge of sadness in its tune. I knew not where it came from and I suspected only little at the time for I did not know your heart then. Your music, the manner in which you had delivered those notes, it was what first turned my eyes in your direction and put meaning in my heart. Something was awakened in me when I heard you play that song, something that hadn't been stirred in a long time. That day, that very moment, I wanted you, Iara. And though I discerned sadness in your heart, I was not wholly convinced for you exhibited no such emotion since that facet of your past had been consigned to oblivion. And when this truth was confirmed in my mind, as it was when you perceived his voice out in the forest on the day of the hunt, I desired to shelter you for as long as I could from the heartache and distress that accompany such loss."

"You were the general who took charge of that brutal assignment?"

"Yes."

"Why did he never mention your name before?"

"Our duties at court encompassed a wide array of tasks, some of which necessitated a high level of secrecy," answered Lord Kessler, "As my second-in-command and dearest friend at court, the secrecy of our friendship was instrumental in achieving many of our goals. He was thus prohibited from speaking of our friendship to everyone, even his sweetheart. I do not deny my hand in causing Lieutenant Vidur's untimely death but I do wish to prove my innocence in this affair with regard to duty and intent. Iara, I shall now relate to you the circumstances of that fateful night you dreamt about in hopes of earning your confidence once more."

XV

The Parting

When I was seventeen years of age, I served as a soldier in the imperial court of Austria. There I met Lieutenant Vidur who was not only my most competent soldier but who also became my closest confidant. He was a brother to me and so was I to him. We pledged a vow of allegiance to each other, a vow signed in blood and sealed with a prayer. Together, we forged fiercely into battle and fought side by side. Providence smiled on us and poured its bountiful blessings upon us so that we were constantly bathed in riches and glory.

"In December of 1827, we were summoned to the palace to hold council with the royal advisors. There we were given explicit instructions to assassinate nine prominent members of the court along with the members of their immediate families and all relations to the second degree. These powerful and high-ranking officials were suspected of conspiring to overthrow the monarchy and our task was to eliminate any threat that they or their relations would pose to the throne. Their vast popularity and influence throughout the region compelled us to orchestrate these executions in secret and with the utmost care. And so the charge was entrusted to me as a matter of great importance and urgency.

"Lieutenant Vidur and I were both loyal members of the court and as such, our devotion to the king extended beyond our official duties. We agreed without hesitation that should we be apprehended during the course of this mission, we would readily confess to the crime of high treason in order to avoid revealing His Majesty's secret plans. The nature of this mission was such that any small error on our part would instantly expose our identities and condemn us to a traitor's death. Hence it was crucial that we carried out the assignment without mercy and without hesitancy so that all would be fulfilled as planned.

"It took us a fortnight to conduct these executions and performed our duty in solemn fashion. On the eve of the fourteenth day, however, our covert undertaking was discovered by members of the royal guard. A single fatal and unavoidable flaw on our part led to our immediate arrest. That night was the worst night of my life. The sorrows of the nights thereafter would not compare to what I felt the night we were arrested. We were brought before the high tribunal and questioned without cease. We were informed that our identities would be protected until the announcement of the verdict was made. Those who had charge over the trial were furious at our unyielding attitude and threatened to have us tortured by cruel means. Still, we remained steadfast in our determination not to disclose any vital details regarding our mission. We were put into a tolerable and decent cell but it was a dungeon of despair nonetheless and when the hour arrived, they came to take him first.

"Just before we parted, Lieutenant Vidur said to me, 'Dearest Nikolas, know that my love for you is infinite and true. I shall deliver us both. I swear we shall meet again in the palace of our true King. Until then, remember us and cherish our friendship.'

"Sadhil Vidur, your beloved, died that night. He was tortured to death inside the palace dungeon. He made that last farewell to you because he knew we would not succeed in this mission and that facing execution was inevitable. The virtues I had upheld so passionately throughout my life shattered as I beheld his noble face in my mind and heard his agonizing cries echoing through the corridor, stifled only by my own cries of mercy for my dear friend.

"I died that night. I died in all but my earthly body. My life ended as Lieutenant Vidur's had ended. I descended into the abyss of hell and kissed the hand of the devil who whispered in my ear, comforting me with empty promises and breathing despair into my wretched heart.

"'Your beloved friend whom you so cherished has been

torn from you this day as if he were torn from your very own flesh. I shall give you recompense for his untimely death. I shall grant you a new life where sorrow will not touch you. Hearken unto my words and never forget your grief. Punish those who have wronged you. Promote strife in they that hurt you. Shame those that laughed in your face as you begged like a dog for mercy. Show the world not the extent of your pity but the magnitude of your wrath. Let your anguish be your weapon. Strike down all your adversaries and seize revenge. Such vengeance is yours if you want it!'

"My wrath was inconsolable for the fire in me could not be contained. I desired retribution above all. I wanted to paint the grounds red with the blood of those hardhearted men who had slaughtered my friend. And so I did. At the lash of my whip they were scourged. They pleaded desperately for clemency but I remained utterly unmoved. Their humiliation was my consolation; their pain, a bandage for my wounds. I reveled in their affliction; every drop of blood delivered by the whip added to my satisfaction. And yet the fire within me could not be quenched, not even when the crack of the whip was no more."

XVI

The Isle of Hope

*T*he immortal rose you possess symbolizes Lieutenant Vidur's undying love for you and the health of this flower is sustained by your love for him," Lord Kessler said, glancing at the jeweled casket on the table.

As Iara reached to take it, he placed his hand over hers and said, "No, give me the rose. It is in desperate want of nourishment. Perhaps I shall be the one to bring it back to life." Then looking intently into her eyes, he added, "I have told you before that securing your happiness is foremost in my thoughts. I would do anything to ensure that you are blessed with the happy life you deserve."

A wave of inconsolable sadness swept over his eyes as he clasped her close to his heart. "This is to be our last embrace before we part. Iara, had I known you were the lover of my dearest friend, I would not have even dreamed of earning your affection. Yet I am grateful for my ignorance for you have given me all the joy I need in this world. Be of good cheer, my sweet. Know that not even death can part us, I will always be with you for ours is an abiding friendship. Tomorrow I shall awaken in perfect peace and with all my wounds completely healed, I promise. And now I have one more confession to make. Since our very first meeting at Hayden Court, I have felt a genuine desire for you accompanied, but not overshadowed, by my friendship with and loyalty to your beloved. My love for you is true and untainted, as love is in its purest form. My heart will always remain yours, Iara."

"I choose you, Nikolas," said Iara.

"What?"

"I love you, Nikolas. Whatever you have done, however dark your past, I still love you. I love you, all of you! Do you hear me?"

He nodded, smiling. "Yes, Iara," said he and folded her tightly in his arms and whispered in her ear, "Bless your heart, dear girl. You are truly an angel. Forever my sweet angel." His voice carried its usual charm and the words enveloped in warmth and romance, yet she discerned in their utterance an undeniable melancholia and for a moment, it seemed as though they had been attended by a stream of silent tears.

"I dreamt of you last night," said Lord Kessler, still holding her in his arms, "I dreamt of us sailing on a raft across the waters of the Pacific. The seas around us were tranquil and inviting; so were the gentle winds that moved our raft. We sailed forever across an endless ocean, away from our European sanctuary and towards a distant Utopia. We spoke without words and laughed without tears and in our eyes, we read each other's heart.

"Then a great darkness came and overshadowed us, turning our joy into fear for it brought with it a vicious gale that shook our raft to and fro. The dark waters seethed beneath us, splashing violently all around, threatening to tear us apart. Our raft was tossed mercilessly in every direction and we were almost thrown into the stygian waters. I looked all around me, over the horizon and beyond, but could not espy land anywhere for the dark had encroached upon the waters with a fury of its own and unleashed in its wrath was the reflection of our souls.

"So dark was the night that I could see nothing at all, not the sky that had shared its light nor the solid raft on which we lay. I could not see your beautiful face, could not hear your sweet voice, could not feel the warmth of your touch. And in my despair, I thought that I had lost you altogether. Then I discerned the sound of your voice coming from afar; it was like the voice of an angel singing in my ears. With a renewed spirit, I left the safety of the raft and swam vigorously towards an uncharted land. I was soon overcome with fatigue but the sound of your sweet voice kept urging me onwards. I soon felt unconscious and drifted off into a deep sleep.

"Suddenly, the skies cleared and the terrible storm that had so tormented us disappeared once and for all. I looked around and saw that I was washed ashore on a beautiful island. A dazzling ray of light beamed from the vault of heaven and surrounded me, enfolding me in a blanket of hope. All around me was pure bliss, such bliss as I had never experienced in my life. I could not erase the smile from my face. I could not force a frown upon my countenance. I was overwhelmed by such great joy that I began to weep. I wept for the both of us because we were now free and could embrace that which we had always treasured.

"Alas, I had rejoiced too early for you were not with me on that island. You were safe on that raft, far from me and deep in your own thoughts. You knew I was gone from you and your tears were relentless. You called to me but I could not come to console you. It saddened me but I never once contemplated going back the way I came, of returning to you. It was not because I did not want to be with you. It was because I did not want you to be with me, at least not yet. In my mind, I saw your face and I saw that look of passion, the one I glimpsed before leaving you on that raft. My happiness was defined by what you felt. Every tear you shed was a strike to my heart. Every time you called my name, I shed a tear. And from my tears, a river sprung.

"For an eternity, I stayed on that island and never once

did the remembrance of you begin to fade or even alter in any way. There your face always shone and the sweet memories I shared with you surrounded me in amaranthine ecstasy. I lived every moment in your arms and kissed you a thousand times each day. We commanded millions of stars to shine upon us and exalted God in our hearts. We remained on that island for all time and never once looked back at the raft that had carried us there. I was in Heaven and you were with me and we were inseparable."

"My sweet Nikolas," said Iara.

"And you are my Iara. Forever, my Iara," declared Lord Kessler, his eyes glistening in the soft candlelight, and leaned his face close to hers and they kissed ever so passionately.

XVII

A Valkuriz Sonata

A sweet melody drifting through the halls of Schloss Valkuriz stirred Iara from her slumber. Entranced by the mesmerizing canvas on which its haunting notes were drawn, she was soon seduced into following it like one deprived of her senses. The strong desire to discover its composer urged her onwards through the dark and lonely halls of the castle, inhabited by the shades of her remembrance. With an eager spirit she pressed on and yet with such leisurely steps she walked for she desired that nothing at all should interrupt the lovely flow of the melody which she knew to be angelic and pure. Its harmony resonated deep within her soul, the romance of ages locked within each individual chord, gently lulling her back to sleep with its angelic flair. But she would not sleep! How could she? A dream within a dream, making sleep so dear...

The chamber door stood half ajar, as if inviting her in. She entered. An empty room it was and dark and gloomy was its ambience. The only piece of furniture was a grand pianoforte, its bench unoccupied, so that it seemed as though the song were being played by a pair of spectral hands. The windows suddenly flew open all around and a strong gust of wind filled the entire room. The curtains shook vigorously in turn, gradually relenting in their pace, slowing to a gentle sway.

Then she saw him. There he was – the pianist sitting at his instrument, immersed in the beauty of his creation and unaware of her presence. His fingers danced gracefully across the keyboard and with each successive note he played came a splash of blood. He played and bled, bled and played, until he was covered in blood and blood was cascading down the sides of the instrument and the streaks of moonlight swirling around him were painted red.

Suddenly, he stopped playing and all was silent within. So enraptured was Iara by the melody which had been play-ing that the new silence now seemed strange to her. She had forgotten altogether its voice, its penetrating gloom. He rose from the bench and turned slowly towards her, his face a shadowy form. Like an apparition he appeared, shrouded by night and encircled by the grim shadows of the grave. He staggered towards her, blood trailing on the floor behind him. He stretched out his hand towards her as if inviting her to share his dismal realm and she saw that her own hands were imbrued with the revenant's blood. The ghostly hand drew nearer so that the ring on its finger was now visible and engraved on the ring was the emblem of Schloss Valkuriz.

Nikolas!

Iara wakened in the dead stillness of night. Sweat trickled down her face yet a sudden chill came over her so that she quickly drew the blanket tight around her body. The dream seemed real, just as her previous dreams had seemed. And just as her previous dreams had proved true in their narration of the past, she feared this one would prove true in its interpretation of the future. Something was amiss, she could sense it. The dream was an omen, a foreboding of sorts, and inherent in its prophecy was a warning of imminent doom. She quickly got out of the bed and wrapped a shawl around herself then took up the candle standing on the table.

As she walked hurriedly through the halls of the castle, she became overwhelmed by a feeling of depression. She stared at the light flickering before her, the faint glimmer of the candle conveying a sense of loneliness. Somewhere in the distance, she heard the clock strike the fourth hour. She was startled by the sound which, though soft and subtle, seemed to take on a deafening tone in the deep stillness of the night.

She knocked on the door of the chamber and when no response came, she opened the door and entered. How very different its atmosphere now seemed from that of the previous night. It was as if a great cloud of gloom had fallen upon the entire room. As she neared the bed, she discerned a series of faint moans. Her heart dropped instantly and she felt a precise pain that begged to be released. Lord Kessler had been awake the whole time.

In her newly resurrected knowledge of her own past, she feared that the truthful recollections delivered by her dreams would confirm the worst of her fears. The dim light of the candle offered only a small reassurance in the dark, a reassurance that did not extend beyond the radius of its illumination. She proceeded further until she touched the foot of the bed and with a trembling hand, she pulled back the curtains. The sight that lay before her brought sheer horror upon her countenance.

XVIII

The Essence of the Rose

*L*ord Kessler was lying in a vast pool of blood on the bed. His ashen face, drenched in a thick mixture of sweat and blood, was barely recognizable. His disheveled hair, dripping wet with perspiration and clumped together as if tousled by the most vicious rain, hung in a mess all over his face. Blood flowed profusely from a gash on the side of his head, spreading fresh paints of crimson on the bloodstained sheets. His clothes were likewise saturated with blood and the numerous wounds on his body were visible through the fabric of his shirt which cleaved to his mutilated form, revealing tiny pieces of flesh that had escaped the confines of his body. An unquenchable fire began first to spread then raged inside of him, its poisonous arrow of unceasing pain shooting through every bone and vessel in his body.

Iara stared at him, transfixed by the ghastly nature of his suffering, her heart heavy and her spirit sinking into utter desolation. In the subdued light of the candle, the unearthly appearance of his being was horrific to behold as his frightfully emaciated frame seemed to take on a new frailty. She fell on him with the gentlest of force and leaned in to kiss his quivering lips, her tears gently washing away the blood from his face.

"My sweet, sweet Nikolas," she whispered in his ear, "I love you with all my heart."

He smiled lovingly at her and in that smile, Iara beheld the most beautiful and radiant soul on earth. Then he closed his eyes and breathed his last.

Tears poured from her eyes as she cradled his lifeless body in her arms, her grief inconsolable. Lord Kessler had blessed her soul with every form of happiness he knew yet had neglected to nurture his own and she, in receiving such blessings, had failed to foresee the deteriorating condition of his spirit. He had offered her generous words of consolation and encouragement at a time when he himself was in need of such comfort. He had spoken to her of erasing her pains, of giving her the happy life she deserved. He had informed her of their last embrace and had graced that final kiss with genuine ardor. He, the master of Schloss Valkuriz, had played the part of a slave; he had indulged her with every comfort he knew and had done so at the expense of his own happiness. Yet she had provided him no avenue of escape from the grief he so patiently and courageously bore but had instead released the dart that had so cruelly pierced his heart and soul.

In Lord Kessler's hand lay the sacred rose. The deathly pallor that had passed over the flower was now gradually fading. Iara recalled the words he had spoken to her just hours ago and understood the meaning of it all. In an effort to secure her own happiness, he had taken unto himself the selfsame wounds of the immortal flower, sacrificing his own life for her pleasure. As such, the affliction that had plagued the rose now plagued his mortal body. And in so doing, his blood had nourished it with life, restoring its crimson so that the flower now glowed with resplendence. And while she gazed upon the mystical flower, a sudden realization dawned on her and she shuddered with fear as she glimpsed the truth about the rose.

The rose was neither sacred nor divine. It was evil. Neither she nor Lieutenant Vidur had known this but Lord Kessler had. He had known it when she recounted the story of her past to him. He had known it when he held the flower in his hand; having once beheld the face of the devil, he was now able to perceive it once more. He had glimpsed it in the rose, in its deathlessness and in the horrifying image of its deterioration, and had sacrificed his life on account of destroying this evil once and for all.

Suddenly, the windows all around flung open and a cold draught passed through the room. Someone was there with her, standing close behind her. She could feel the specter's breath on her neck, its breath cold against the warmth of her skin. Very slowly she turned around and saw him – the mysterious soldier in the portrait, the familiar stranger in the woods, the man who invaded her dreams… her lover.

Lieutenant Vidur stood before her as handsome as ever, just as he was in life, just as he was in her dreams. Yet in the argent glow of the moon, she beheld a sinister aspect in his eyes and drew back in fear.

"Why are you afraid of me, my princess?" he asked, eyes glinting, "Do I make your blood run cold? I am not frightening to look upon, am I? I come to you not as I was when I breathed my last but as I was when I walked the earth. Are you not overjoyed to reunite with your dearly beloved?"

"Sadhil –"

"Tell me, my love, when they chained me to the rack, did you ask God to intercede on my behalf? When they tore the very limbs from my body, did you shed a single tear for my sake? When they dragged my mangled corpse through the desolate marshland to be left as carrion for vultures, did you even look back and give me a moment's thought? And now when General Kessler sacrifices his precious life for you, you grieve for him so passionately," and touching the tears on Iara's face, said, "Even now, you lament his death and not mine."

"You were his most cherished friend at court," Iara said through the veil of tears that shrouded her eyes.

"And I thought the world of him," replied the lieutenant,

"I was his most loyal subordinate and served him ever so dutifully. And when the dark hour came upon us, I surrendered my life so that his could be spared. I loved him, Iara, just as I loved you." Then he drew even nearer towards her and held her face firmly in his hands.

"Kiss me, sweetheart," said he, "Kiss me like you kissed your beloved Nikolas. Come into my arms and be with me forever, my darling. It is what you want, isn't it?"

"You are not the man I once loved," she said, "You cannot be. Your words are cold and full of hate. Your eyes are cruel and unforgiving. Your touch is like a serpent's –"

"Shh," he said, putting his finger on her lips, "Wipe away your tears, princess. The time for mourning is over."

*D*awn came as it had always come and with it the crisp scent of morning dew. The sun shone as brilliantly as always yet there was a darkness in its glow and such darkness overshadowed the castle of Schloss Valkuriz. The pretty flowers lining the garden path danced elegantly in the wind, swaying to the rhythm of life. New buds blossomed for the first time and peered upwards at the sky while the flowers of old bowed their heads and touched the ground. The songbirds nestling among the leaves sang that morning with all their natural grace but their songs possessed little cheer and much gloom. In short, everything was as tradition had ordained yet nothing was as it had been.

At nine o'clock that morning, servants entered Lord Kessler's chamber to attend to their master as was their custom. Much to their surprise and grief, they beheld the corpse of their beloved master as they drew back the bed curtains. Lying close beside him was Iara, her body wrapped lovingly around his and her gown soaked in blood. And just as they mourned the loss of their master, so too did the servants mourn the loss of his sweetheart. A sword with cerulean diamonds embellished on the hilt and stained with blood lay on the floor near the bed. And in Lord Kessler's hand was a beautiful red rose.

The End